Dear Parent:

YO-AQX-460

In this charming story, Emily Elizabeth learns a lesson that many of us take a lifetime to acquire: We can count our true friends on the fingers of one hand. A true friend is someone who believes in you and stands by you—no matter what. A true friend doesn't waver when less loyal buddies succumb to the social pressure of turning away. It's easy to be a fair-weather friend, but challenging to be a true and loyal one. And it's as important to *be* one as it is to have one. In *The Doggy Detectives*, Clifford and T-Bone stand up to the doubters and prove to be Emily Elizabeth's loyal friends.

Young children face similar challenges to their loyalties. When, for example, the members of a self-appointed "in" crowd of preschoolers or primary graders decide not to play with some hapless child, and urge others to join them, friendships are severely tested. Sometimes a child is forced to choose between two friends. "I won't play with you anymore if you play with him," is an all-too-common threat. You might expect your child to rise to the occasion and say, "If you want to play with me, you have to include **X** because both of you are my friends." Don't be disappointed, however, if this doesn't happen. It takes time to feel socially confident enough to take this stand. Even adults waffle in similar situations, and many regretfully recall such scenes from childhood.

When your child is confronted with such a challenge, sharing stories of similar situations can be very helpful—provided you don't portray yourself as having been conflict-free and noble at all times. Let your child know you've been there, understand the struggle, and provide some prudent guidance.

Adele M. Brodkin, Ph.D.

Visit Clifford at scholastic.com/clifford

ISBN 0-439-41196-3

Library of Congress Cataloging-in-Publication Data is available

10 9 8 7 6 5 4 3 2   01 02 03 04 05 06

Printed in the U.S.A.   24
First printing, June 2001

Clifford THE BIG RED DOG®

The Doggy Detectives

Adapted by David L. Harrison

Illustrated by José Maria Cardona

Based on the Scholastic book series "Clifford The Big Red Dog" by Norman Bridwell

From the television script "To Catch a Bird" by Meg McLaughlin

SCHOLASTIC INC.

New York   Toronto   London   Auckland   Sydney   Mexico City
New Delhi   Hong Kong

When Jetta won the spelling bee,
She bragged and bragged to Emily.
"My medal is a gorgeous sight!
Watch it glisten in the light!

Emily, hide my spelling prize

While I play soccer with the guys.

I'm trusting you to hide my gold

In case some thief is feeling bold."

A crow as crafty as could be
Was watching Jetta from a tree.
"I'm so sly she'll never know
Who stole her medal," said the crow.

He chuckled with a greedy caw,
Flew so fast that no one saw,
Stole the gold without a sound,
And no one knew he'd been around.

When Jetta put her sweater on.
She cried, "Oh, no! My medal's gone!
Who took it, Mac? Do you know who?
I bet I know! And you do, too!"

"Emily Elizabeth, give it back!

I know you took it! So does Mac!

You're jealous just because I won!

What a terrible thing you've done!"

"Jetta, I would never steal!

You don't know how bad I feel!

Perhaps you lost it coming here.

Perhaps your medal's very near."

Above them laughed the crafty crow,

"Just how near, you'll never know!"

"We know Emily's not to blame!
It's up to us to clear her name!"

"How do we prove it?
What do we use?"

"Detectives always look for clues.
We'll start by sniffing around the park."

"And if we find a clue,
We'll bark!"

"That thief had better watch his tail

Now that we are on his trail!

This feather makes me sneeze, *AH-CHOO!*"

"T-Bone, try to find a clue!"

"A shiny mirror!" said the crow.

"I'll steal this, too, before they know.

I'll add this mirror to my gold.

Shiny mirrors make me bold!"

"Emily, what is wrong with you?
Now you took my mirror, too!"

"Jetta, why do you think I'd lie?
I feel so bad that I could cry!"

"Emily did it again!" said Mac.

"She won't give Jetta's mirror back."

"She didn't take it!" Clifford howled.

Mac just looked at him and scowled.

"Clifford, what if she really hid

The gold and mirror? Maybe she did!"

"She didn't!" Clifford said with a shout.

"Now hurry! Time is running out!"

"I just hope we're not too late.

We'll use your shiny bow for bait.

And when we catch the thief, you'll see

You're wrong to blame my Emily!"

"Clifford! Look! See what I meant?
Your Emily is not innocent!
She's going to steal my shiny bow!
Admit it, Clifford. Now we know."

"Cleo, dear, you've lost your bow.

Let me help before I go.

Poor Jetta needs me with her now.

We've got to find her things somehow."

The crow appeared but no one saw.

And no one heard his greedy caw.

He stole the bow and no one knew,

But this time T-Bone found the clue.

"My bow is missing!"
Cleo howled.
"She took it after all!"
she scowled.

"She didn't take it!"
Clifford sighed.

"I found a feather!"
T-Bone cried.

Look up there! You see that crow?
We've seen that crow before, you know.
We've found his feathers very near
To where Jetta's things would disappear!

"Jetta, are you satisfied?

Now you know I never lied."

"I was wrong, I realize!

Forgive me! I apologize!"

Mac and Cleo,
What about you?

Whimper! Whine!
We're sorry, too!

"Good old Clifford! Good old friend!
You proved my innocence in the end!"

BOOKS IN THIS SERIES:

Welcome to Birdwell Island: Everyone on Birdwell Island thinks that Clifford is just too big! But when there's an emergency, Clifford The Big Red Dog teaches everyone to have respect—even for those who are different.

A Puppy to Love: Emily Elizabeth's birthday wish comes true: She gets a puppy to love! And with her love and kindness, Clifford The Small Red Puppy becomes Clifford The Big Red Dog!

The Big Sleep Over: Clifford has to spend his first night without Emily Elizabeth. When he has trouble falling asleep, his Birdwell Island friends work together to make sure that he—and everyone else—gets a good night's sleep.

No Dogs Allowed: No dogs in Birdwell Island Park? That's what Mr. Bleakman says—before he realizes that sharing the park with dogs is much more fun.

An Itchy Day: Clifford has an itchy patch! He's afraid to go to the vet, so he tries to hide his scratching from Emily Elizabeth. But Clifford soon realizes that it's better to be truthful and trust the person he loves most—Emily Elizabeth.

The Doggy Detectives: Oh, no! Emily Elizabeth is accused of stealing Jetta's gold medal—and then her shiny mirror! But her dear Clifford never doubts her innocence and, with his fellow doggy detectives, finds the real thief.

Follow the Leader: While playing follow-the-leader with Clifford and T-Bone, Cleo learns that playing fair is the best way to play!

The Big Red Mess: Clifford tries to stay clean for the Dog of the Year contest, but he ends up becoming a big red mess! However, when Clifford helps the judge reach the shore safely, he finds that he doesn't need to stay clean to be the Dog of the Year.

The Big Surprise: Poor Clifford. It's his birthday, but none of his friends will play with him. Maybe it's because they're all busy. . . planning his surprise party!

The Wild Ice Cream Machine: Charley and Emily Elizabeth decide to work the ice cream machine themselves. Things go smoothly. . . until the lever gets stuck and they find themselves knee-deep in ice cream!

Dogs and Cats: Can dogs and cats be friends? Clifford, T-Bone, and Cleo don't think so. But they have a change of heart after they help two lost kittens find their mother.

The Magic Ball: Emily Elizabeth trusts Clifford to deliver a package to the post office, but he opens it and breaks the gift inside. Clifford tries to hide his blunder, but Emily Elizabeth appreciates honesty and understands that accidents happen.